Kisses for brave Jack!

BRAVE JACK

NAUGHTY LION

Bien Venue!

Uncle Henry & Jack having a lovely day at the seaside! xx

To Theo, an inspiration! - J.J

For Uncle Mark, with all my love - E.W

First published in 2008
by Hodder Children's Books

Text copyright © Julia Jarman 2008
Illustration copyright © Erica-Jane Waters 2008

Hodder Children's Books
338 Euston Road
London NW1 3BH

Hodder Children's Books Australia
Level 17/207 Kent Street
Sydney, NSW 2000

A catalogue record of this book is available
from the British Library.

ISBN: 978 0 340 94481 3
10 9 8 7 6 5 4 3 2 1

Printed in China

Hodder Children's Books
is a division of Hachette Children's Books
An Hachette Livre UK Company

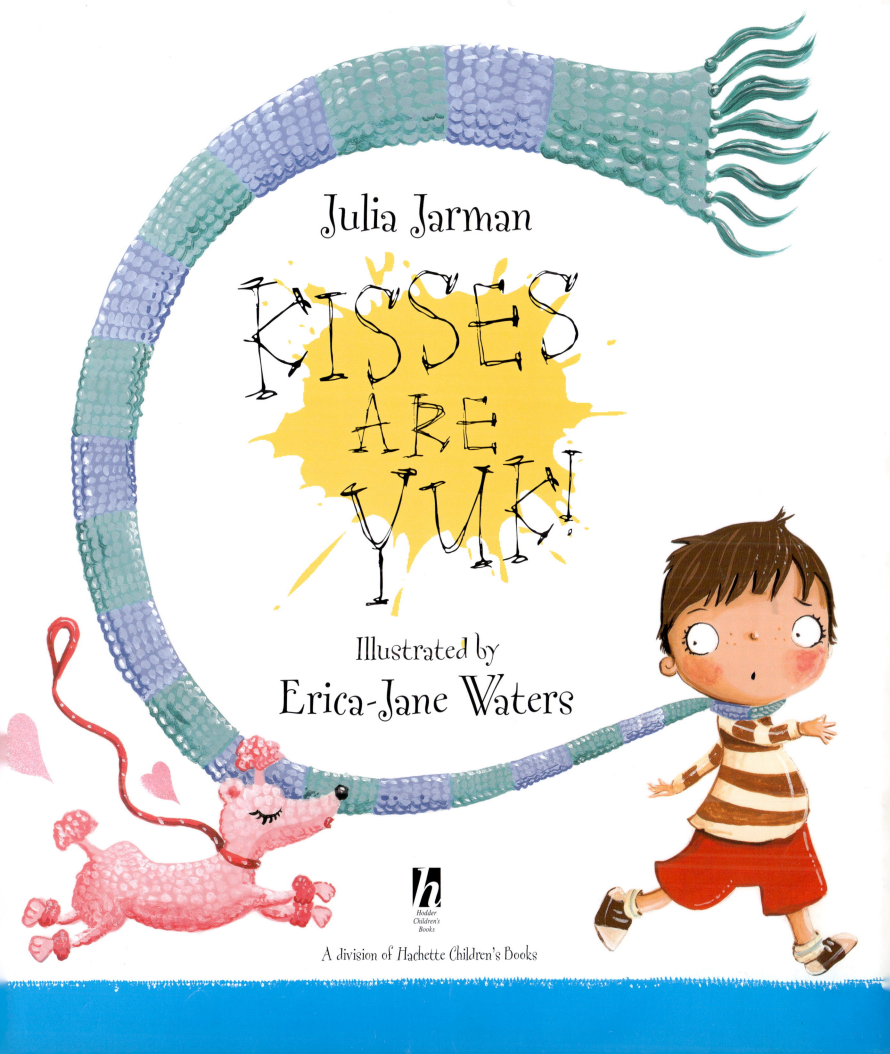

Julia Jarman

KISSES ARE YUK!

Illustrated by

Erica-Jane Waters

Hodder Children's Books

A division of Hachette Children's Books

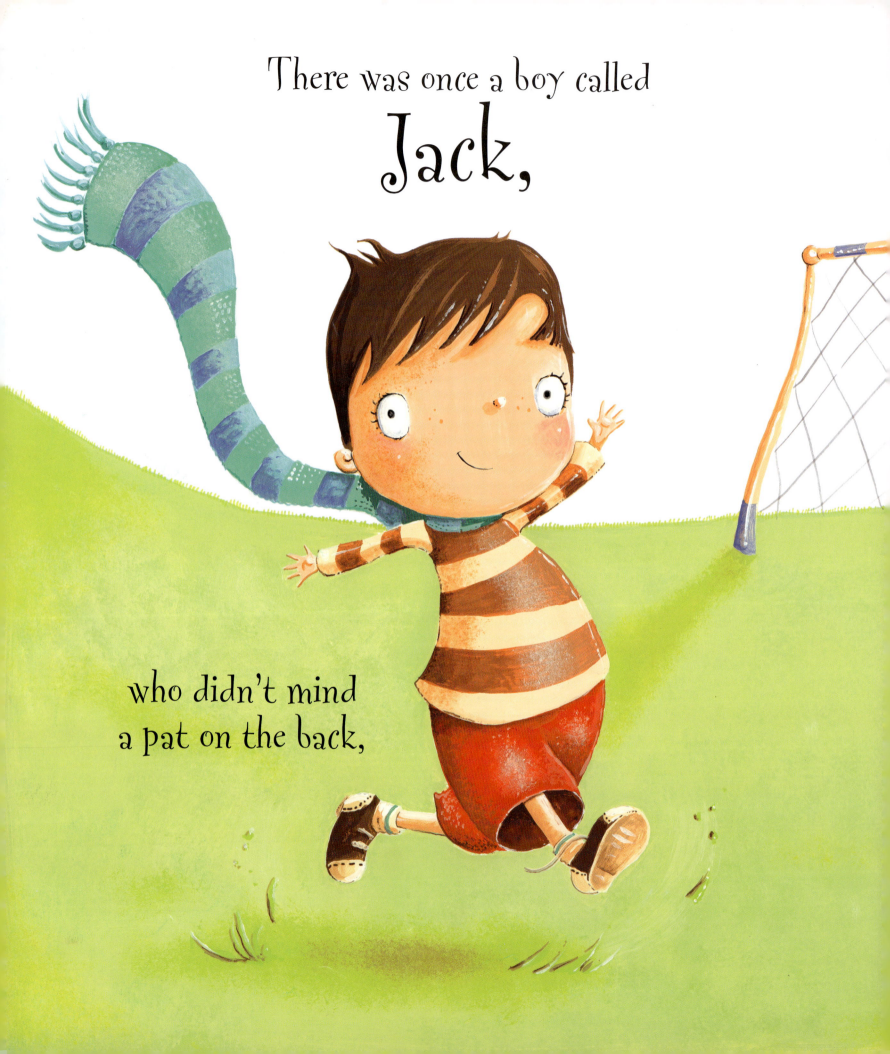

There was once a boy called
Jack,

who didn't mind
a pat on the back,

when he scored **a great goal,**

or **jumped** over a pole,

but...

he thought
kisses were
YUK!

He didn't mind a manly
handshake,
when he saved Sue
from the lake,

or when
he saved Klaus
from a burning
house,

but...

he thought kisses were
MUCK!

He quite liked a
'Very well done!
I'm really proud
of you, son,'

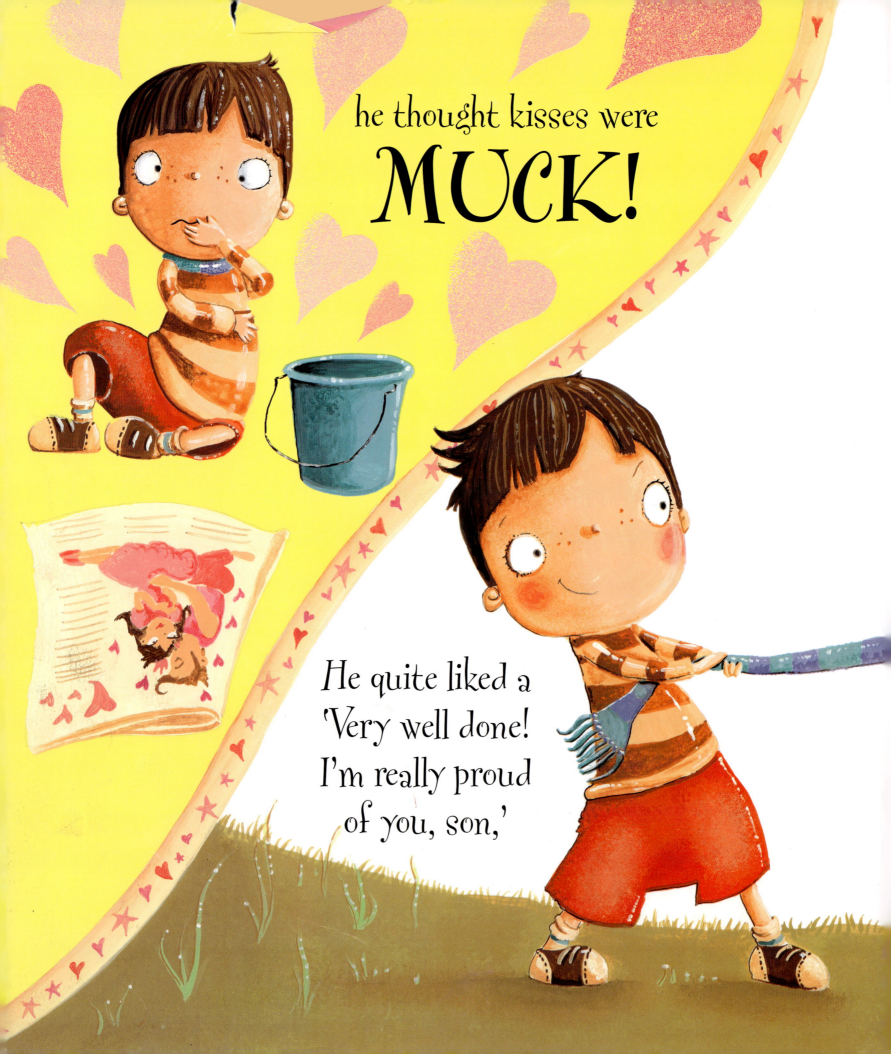

when he rescued Brian
from the jaws of a lion.

He loved getting prizes
and
cups
of **all**
sizes,

but...

DANGER!!
WET ROAD
AHEAD!

kisses were yukky,
kisses were sucky,
kisses were
very,
very
UNLUCKY!

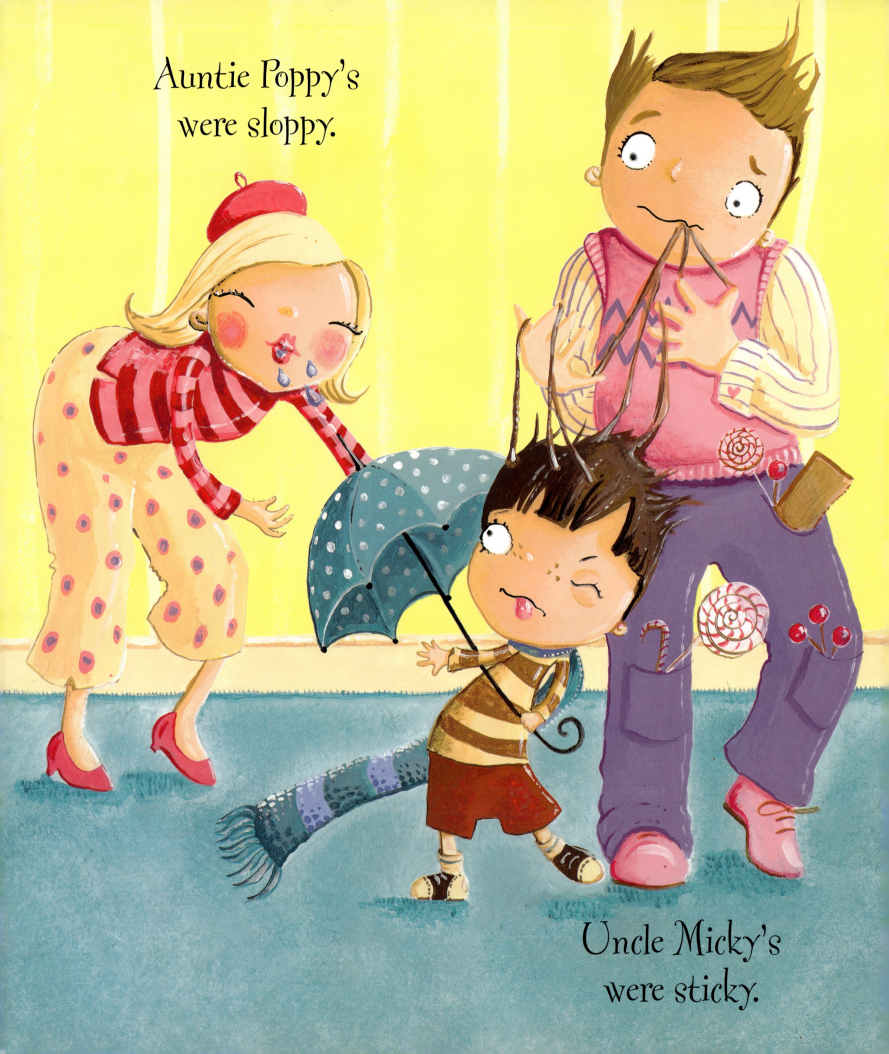

Auntie Poppy's
were sloppy.

Uncle Micky's
were sticky.

Cousin Lily's were horribly licky.

Uncle Henry's were hairy.
Auntie Mary's were scary.

And being kissed
by Great Uncle Russ
was like being kissed
by a very stiff brush.

Uncle Sam
did smackeroos.

Tante Èclaire,
she kissed
in twos.

Granny Groover
kissed
like a hoover.

But worst
of all was
Auntie
Rhonda.

She
kissed
like
an...

anaconda!

So, one night,
Jack made up a rule:
ABSOLUTELY
NO
KISSES
at all...

or stroking my hair,

or poking my tum, or squeezing my knees, or patting my bum.

He stuck the new law on his bedroom door. 'Read that, if you can!' Signed by 'macho man!'

'I'm big and **strong.**

I'm brave and **tough.**

WORLD'S TOUGHEST

Mess
with me
and
I'll get
rough!'

Then Jack
climbed into
bed and snuggled
down with...

Growly Ted
and Furry Dog
and Velvet Rabbit,

for cuddling was his secret habit.

And – **PLEASE** don't tell anyone –
he didn't mind...

a kiss from Mum!

KISSUS
sloppious

Kissus
stickious

Kyssus
grannious

Kissus
hairious

Kissus
frenchious

Kissus
caninious

S.W.A.L.K.